J^E
c.1

CL _{DEC} '90

SHAZAM!

LORNA KENT

Viking Kestrel

One morning in the garden
As we were planting seeds
We found an old and rusty chest
All overgrown with weeds

"This chest is full of hats," cried Dad
"Come here and have a look!"
And as he took one from the top
We found a magic book

Choose the hat you like the best
And place it on your head
Now say the magic word aloud
The dusty spell book read

rn the page and you'll find out
e special magic word to shout…

SHAZAM!

Then Mummy found a golden crown
She put it on her head
And suddenly our beans on toast
Were something else instead

Say it loudly if you can
The special magic word...

SHAZAM!

"Oh, look, a play chest full of hats
What fun!" said Uncle Joe
He tried a spaceman's helmet on
I wonder where we'll go?

Say it loudly if you can
The special magic word…

SHAZAM!

As we made castles in the sand
Our Auntie sipped her tea
"This is a funny hat," she laughed
"Does it look good on me?"

Say it loudly if you can
The special magic word…

SHAZAM!

Grandpa made our bathtime fun
He sprayed us with the shower
He didn't know the pirate hat
Was filled with magic power

Say it loudly if you can
The special magic word...

SHAZAM!

"It's my turn next," our Grandma said
And as we read our book
She tried a witch's black hat on
We couldn't bear to look

Say it loudly if you can
the special magic word…

SHAZAM!

"It's getting late," our Daddy said
And pointed to our beds
We quickly took the last two hats
And put them on our heads

Whisper softly if you can
The special magic word...

Shazam!

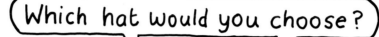

For Nigel

VIKING KESTREL
Published by the Penguin Group
Viking Penguin Inc., 40 West 23rd Street, New York, New York 10010, U.S.A.
27 Wrights Lane, London W8 5TZ, England
Penguin Books Australia Ltd, Ringwood, Victoria, Australia
Penguin Books Canada Ltd, 2801 John Street, Markham, Ontario, Canada L3R 1B4
Penguin Books (N.Z.) Ltd, 182-190 Wairau Road, Auckland 10, New Zealand

Penguin Books Ltd, Registered Offices: Harmondsworth, Middlesex, England

First published in Great Britain 1989 by
Hamish Hamilton Children's Books

First published in the U.S.A. by Viking Kestrel 1989

1 3 5 7 9 8 6 4 2

Text and illustrations copyright © 1989 by Lorna Kent

ISBN 0-670-83073-9

Printed in Great Britain by
Cambus Litho, East Kilbride